Dedicated to the hopes and dreams of children everywhere.

Contact us at:

DantheFish9@gmail.com

Wade the Turtle

By Daniel Gebhart, Cathie Gebhart, & Wade Keller

Illustrated by Haley Anderson   *Book Design by* Christian M. Wehr

Summer was finally here. Wade loved summertime. He was a great swimmer, and when the weather got hot, everyone headed to the pond to swim. The only problem was that in order to get to the pond, Wade had to cross the street. This didn't seem to be a problem for Wade's friends. They just waited until the road was clear and ran across.

But crossing the road didn't come as easily to Wade. No matter how much he concentrated, his short turtle legs could not speed up to run across the hot pavement. Still, swimming was something Wade did best. He knew if he could just get to the pond, this summer would be wonderful.

Wade started to cross, keeping his head up and his eyes on the far side of the road. The heat of the asphalt bothered his feet, but he knew it would be worth it. One step, one step, one step. Suddenly a car roared overhead, forcing Wade inside his protective shell. When Wade was scared, he always found comfort inside his shell. It was hard to come out again, to know when it was safe to try. But eventually, Wade poked out his head and saw the coast was clear.

Halfway there. The swimming hole was in reach when another car headed straight toward him. Wade hid in his shell, hoping to feel safe. He heard the car slow down, and the door creak open. The driver said, "Poor little turtle, let me help you."

Wade felt himself being lifted off the heated road and placed in the cool green grass. "This feels good," Wade thought as he heard the car pull away.

Coming out of his shell, Wade's spirits fell. The driver had placed him on the wrong side of the road; he was back at the beginning of his journey.

Wade could hear happy voices laughing from the pond. Tears welled in Wade's eyes as he thought that he would never be able to swim with his friends. "I hate summer," Wade said, looking with longing at the far side of the road once again.

Wade didn't see the boy on the bike riding up the road, but the boy saw Wade. "Hi, little turtle," said the boy. "Are you going swimming, too?" The boy had a towel draped over the handles of his bike and the happiness of someone enjoying a summer day.

Wade tried to smile, thinking of the long trek across the road. "I am a very good swimmer," said Wade.

"I am sure you are," replied the boy. "Come swim with me." The boy parked his bike, scooped up Wade, and crossed the street to the pond. The turtle and the boy spent the afternoon swimming and playing in the summer sun.

"I love summer," thought Wade.

Wade the Boy

There are some things I can't do. Like open those stupid ketchup packets without getting it all over my shirt. Sometimes I think I hate ketchup, but have you tried to eat a school lunch without it?

My mom had a list from the doctor of all the things I could never do. I surprised everyone since I can do everything on the list. (Opening a ketchup packet wasn't on the list.) I won't be a brain surgeon (but I don't like blood anyway) and the National Guard recruiter said I couldn't join because of the palsy, but other than that (and the ketchup), I am good to go.

I have an aide at school. She is okay, but sometimes it is hard to be the only kid with this extra person just hanging around.

Kids aren't allowed to call people "stupid" or "retard" if the teacher is around, but when they say, "you're special," in a way that means stupid or retard, the teacher doesn't say anything. Sometimes I can just shake it off, other times not so much.

Sometimes people try to help me, but it doesn't help at all. I think people try to be nice, but they can make me feel stupid. I just want to do the same things as everyone else. I like it when people do things with me, not for me. I really can learn how to do it if someone shows me what to do.

Nice people that don't help are better than mean people that just try to make me cry. When I am around mean people, I just want to go home and never come out again.

Wade the Inspiration

Wade was born and raised in Mobridge, South Dakota and is a 1999 graduate of Mobridge High School. He continues to root for all the sports at the school, traveling with the high school football and basketball teams as their manager. Wade loves to swim and is a regular at the city pool.

Wade works at Payless Foods, helping people get their groceries bagged and to their cars. He won Mobridge Employee of the Year in 2007. In addition, he travels each summer having different experiences including being a volunteer umpire assistant at the annual Ripken World Series in Aberdeen, MD. Wade loves sports, especially his teams: the Cubs, the Bulls, and the Broncos.

Wade writes, "I feel bad for people who are bullied. I think bullying needs to be stopped." When Wade found out that Dan was bullied in school, he wanted to help write this series of books and said we could use his name for Wade the Turtle.

The section called Wade the Boy is a combination of experiences of several different people including Wade.

Haley the Illustrator

Haley Anderson is a 15 year old student at Boone High School in Iowa. Haley loves art and wants to study art in college. She dreams of being a famous artist. Haley is a member of her high school's Thespian Troupe and helps design sets for the stage. Haley also loves animals. Haley was born with Treacher Collins syndrome. This syndrome affects 1 in 50,000 people. This syndrome has given Haley many challenges, but she is not going to let it hold her back.

Daniel the Author

Daniel Gebhart has dyslexia and is an advocate for changing people's view towards learning disabilities. After struggling through elementary and middle school, Dan changed his approach to learning and graduated high school in the top of his class without extra assistance. He is an avid board game player/collector and owns seven games that are just zombie themed. He lives in Phoenix, Arizona with his wife, two cats and lots of stuffed Pokemon.

Thank you to everyone who helped this series change from a possibility to a reality. Love and peace to all!

Made in the USA
Middletown, DE
30 November 2016